CONTENTS

1   Off to Fort William Henry 5

2   A New Guide 10

3   Captured! 18

4   Magua's Plan 24

5   A Daring Rescue 30

6   Back at the Fort 36

7   A Terrible Attack 42

8   Duncan's Plan 48

9   The Race of the Captives.............. 56

10 The Bear Magician 63

11 Another Daring Rescue 68

12 A Day of Sorrow 74

SADDLEBACK *Classics*

The Last of the Mohicans

JAMES FENIMORE COOPER

ADAPTED BY

Emily Hutchinson

SADDLEBACK
PUBLISHING · INC.

The Count of Monte Cristo

Gulliver's Travels

The Hound of the Baskervilles

The Jungle Book

The Last of the Mohicans

Oliver Twist

The Prince and the Pauper

The Three Musketeers

Development and Production: Laurel Associates, Inc.
Cover and Interior Art: Black Eagle Productions

SADDLEBACK PUBLISHING, INC.
Three Watson
Irvine, CA 92618-2767

E-Mail: info@sdlback.com
Website: www.sdlback.com

ISBN 1-56254-293-1

Printed in the United States of America
05 04 03   9 8 7 6 5 4 3 2 1

§1 Off to Fort William Henry

It was 1757, the third year of the French and Indian War in America. England and France were fighting for possession of a country that neither one was destined to have. Some Indians were helping the English. Other Indians were helping the French.

A wide, thick forest separated the American settlements of France and England. Both armies had built forts at different points in the forest. As the war went on, these forts were taken and retaken, torn down, and built up again. Colonel Munro commanded the soldiers at Fort William Henry, the largest of the English forts. His young daughters, Cora and Alice, lived with him in one of the houses there.

Both girls were beautiful, but in different ways. Cora, the older one, had shining black hair and dark eyes. Alice had blond hair and blue eyes. They were both as nice to be with as they were beautiful.

As our story opens, Cora and Alice were on their way back to Fort William Henry after visiting friends many miles away. They were being escorted by Major Duncan Heyward, a soldier under Colonel Munro's command. Major Heyward liked both girls —but he was secretly in love with Alice. He had found two good horses for Cora and Alice to ride. And he had brought along his Indian scout, Magua, to show them the way. Alice did not like Magua, but Duncan had insisted that he was a good scout and could be trusted.

Just as the four riders were about to start off, a man rode up. He was tall, thin, and very strange looking. It appeared that his horse was not big enough for him, and even his clothes were too small. He looked as if he didn't know how to ride a horse—and the horse looked just as confused!

The girls, who were very kind, tried hard not to laugh. Duncan asked, "Who are you, sir?"

The thin stranger smiled. "I am a singing teacher," he answered.

"A singing teacher!" Major Heyward could not believe his ears. "But my good man—everyone knows how to sing! What is your *work*?"

"Why, I teach people how to sing," the thin man

repeated. "Surely that is enough to do."

Major Heyward didn't like that answer. He thought that with a war going on a man should do something more important than teach singing.

"May I ride with you to Fort William Henry?" the singing teacher asked timidly. He sounded afraid. "The woods are full of Indians, you know, and I don't know how to fight."

Major Heyward sighed. He didn't want to take care of the singing teacher. It was enough to watch out for Cora and Alice. But Alice said, "Let him come, Duncan." And he could never say no to Alice.

They hadn't gone far when Major Heyward thought he saw a faint gleam in the trees. Could it be a reflection off the glistening eyes of a prowling Indian? He nervously looked over at Magua, who seemed very calm. So Heyward relaxed and smiled to himself. "It must have only been some shiny berries," he thought. "Otherwise Magua would have noticed it, too."

After Major Heyward's party rode on, however, an Indian stepped out from the bushes. He was a Huron, and he was painted for war. The Huron stood silently and looked down the trail, watching his intended victims.

Magua knew the Hurons were watching them. But he did not know that the dense woods held three other men as well.

One of the three was a most unusual white man named Hawkeye. He was a scout for the English. Hawkeye was tall and muscular, made strong by many hardships and long years of hard work. His simple clothes were made from the skins of deer. The sun had browned his face, and time had put a little gray in his hair. The most remarkable thing about Hawkeye, however, was that he had always lived in the woods. For this reason, he knew the woods every bit as well as any Indian did.

The other two men were Indians—but they were not Hurons. They were the only remaining members of a different tribe. Chingachgook and his son, Uncas, were the last of the great Mohicans.

The Mohicans did not wear many clothes. Their bodies were painted all over in shades of white and black. They wore just one long band of hair on their closely shaved heads. Decorated with feathers, this band was left there for their enemies to scalp—if they could.

This day in the woods Chingachgook was sitting on a mossy log. Near him was a deer that Uncas had killed with an arrow. Hawkeye was standing by, filling his powder horn.

As the men talked, Uncas put his ear to the ground. "The horses of white men are coming!" he warned. "Hawkeye, they are your brothers! You must speak to them."

2   A New Guide

When Major Heyward's party came to the clearing, Hawkeye called out, "Who are you?"

"We are friends to the law and to the king," Heyward said as he rode forward. "Will you help us, sir? We are on our way to Fort William Henry, but our Indian guide says he is lost."

"What? An *Indian* lost in the woods!" Hawkeye laughed. "That is very strange. Are you sure your Indian guide is not working for the French?"

"He was born a Huron, but he has lived with the Mohawks. Now he is with us—as a friend," said Heyward.

"He may have lived with the Mohawks for a while. But don't be fooled, man: *Once a Huron, always a Huron*. It's a wonder you still have your scalps," said Hawkeye.

"Really?" asked Major Heyward, looking bewildered. "I *did* think it strange that he lost his way. What do you think I should do now?"

"Just go back to him and keep him talking," Hawkeye suggested. "Uncas and Chingachgook will come around behind him and take him by surprise."

Major Heyward remained calm as he rode back down the trail. When he passed Cora and Alice, he smiled at them. He was pleased that they didn't suspect they were in danger.

Magua was standing with his back against a tree when Major Heyward galloped up to him and said, "Good news! I met a hunter who knows where we are. He will take us to Fort William Henry."

Magua fixed his glowing eyes on Heyward for a long moment. Then he asked, "Is he alone?"

Major Heyward was not accustomed to lying, but he didn't want Magua to know about Uncas and Chingachgook. "Why no," he said, "for we are with him now."

"Then I will leave," said Magua. "The pale faces will see only their own color."

"*Leave?* Then what will you say to Colonel Munro about his daughters? You promised to be their guide. Don't forget that Munro promised you a gift for your services."

Something about Major Heyward's tone made

Magua wonder. Had the English officer found out that he was not really a friend?

Major Heyward was angry. Wanting to capture Magua himself, he got off his horse and went up to the Huron. But as Heyward approached, Magua darted away and ran into the woods.

Chingachgook and Uncas ran after Magua. A moment later, the woods were lighted up by the sudden flash of Hawkeye's rifle.

Blood spattered the bushes where Magua had been running. But even though the Huron had been injured, he had gotten away. Major Heyward wanted to go after him. "We are four able bodies against one wounded man!" he cried out.

"No!" said Hawkeye, holding him back. "I never should have fired my rifle within sound of an ambush! But I couldn't help myself. We'd better get out of here soon—or our scalps will be drying in the wind by tomorrow!"

"What is to be done?" asked Major Heyward, realizing the danger. "The young ladies cannot travel as fast as we can. Won't you stay and help me defend them? You can name your own reward!"

"Spare your offers of money," said Hawkeye. "It has never been of any use to me. But the Mohicans and I will help you—on one condition."

"Name it," said Major Heyward.

"You must never tell anyone about the place where we shall take you," said Hawkeye.

"I will do as you say," Heyward promised.

"Then follow—for we are losing precious time," Hawkeye commanded.

Major Heyward went over to Cora and Alice. He explained what had happened with Magua. He told them that Hawkeye would be their new guide.

Hawkeye's plan was to take Heyward's party down the river by canoe. But he wanted Magua to think that they had taken off on their horses. That way, Magua and the Hurons would go off in the wrong direction looking for them.

Uncas and Chingachgook hid the horses behind some rocks by the river. They tied them to a tree and left them standing in the water.

Then Hawkeye led Heyward, the girls, and the singing teacher down to the river. Before long they came to his hidden canoe. As soon as Cora and Alice were seated, Hawkeye and Heyward pushed the canoe into the deeper water. Then the singing teacher hopped in.

Soon they came to a turn in the river. There

they saw a waterfall that was amazingly high and wide. The water at the top actually seemed to be piled against the heavens! It tumbled into the caverns below with a deafening noise.

Hawkeye directed Heyward and the others to sit in the front of the canoe. Then he paddled directly toward the center of the waterfall!

The passengers looked ahead in horror. They were sure they would be swept overboard! Alice covered her eyes and held her breath. But finally the canoe floated up to the side of a flat rock.

"Where are we?" asked Heyward.

"We're at the foot of Glenn's Falls," Hawkeye answered. "Now we must make a steady landing. Then I'll go back and get the Mohicans."

Hawkeye and Major Heyward helped the others out of the canoe. As the last foot touched the rock, Hawkeye paddled back out into the swirling river.

Soon Hawkeye came back with Uncas and Chingachgook. Then he led Major Heyward and his party into a narrow, deep cavern in the rock. There, Hawkeye quickly made a fire. Then he began to cook a haunch of the deer that Uncas had killed and butchered that day.

The travelers sat by the fire to warm their hands before they ate. By the flickering firelight, they got their first good look at Uncas. "I could sleep in peace," Alice whispered to Cora, "with such a strong and fearless youth for my guard."

Duncan Heyward heard her. "Let us hope that he does not disappoint us," he said.

Then Duncan turned to Hawkeye. "Are we safe here?" he asked.

Hawkeye laughed and nodded. "Such old foxes as Chingachgook and I do not get caught in a burrow with one hole," he said. "Once this island was solid rock. But the water worked this hole for us to hide in. The waterfall is on both sides of us here. The river runs both behind us and in front of us. Yes—we will be safe here."

Uncas handed food and water to Cora and Alice—but he seemed to take a little better care of Cora. He could scarcely keep his dark eyes off her lovely face.

On the other hand, Hawkeye's quick eyes never rested at all. He would stop eating to listen. Then he would stop listening to look. "Come, friend," he said at last to the singing teacher. "Have some of this fresh spring water. It will wash away bad times. What is your name?"

"Gamut—David Gamut," the man said.

"What do you do?" Hawkeye asked.

"I teach the art of singing."

"Can you use a rifle?"

"Thanks be to God, *no*!" David cried.

Hawkeye tried not to laugh. Shaking his head in wonder, he said, "It is a strange way to live—to go about like a bird while other men work!"

Then suddenly, a cry was heard from outside. The sound was neither earthly nor human! The strange cry was followed by a deep stillness.

David was terrified. He jumped up and ran to

the mouth of the cave. Hawkeye called him back
and started after him. But it was too late. Loud
cracks of rifle fire filled the air—and David fell to
the ground. His head had been grazed by a bullet.

# 3 Captured!

Hawkeye shot back. A fierce yell from the other side of the river proved that Hawkeye's bullet had found a victim. After this, the wild cries and the rifle fire stopped.

Duncan Heyward ran to David and carried him back into the cave.

"Is he dead?" Cora gasped in horror.

"He is alive," said Hawkeye. "Let him rest. The longer he sleeps, the better it will be for him. Singing won't do us any good against the Hurons."

"Will they return?" Heyward asked.

Hawkeye laughed. "They lost a man. That's the only reason they fell back just now. But they will come after us again."

The men stood watch during the night. Toward dawn, Duncan began to think that the Hurons had gone away. He asked Hawkeye what he thought.

"They will not give up the chase so easily,"

Hawkeye warned. "Keep your eyes open or your hair will be lost!"

A few moments later, Duncan saw five Hurons coming down the waterfall toward the island. As he watched, one of the Hurons got caught up in the swift current. Duncan could see him reach out for help. But in less than a minute, the man was swept over the falls and seen no more. The other four Hurons made it safely to the island.

"*Hurons!*" Uncas yelled.

"Get ready for attack!" Hawkeye called to Duncan.

Just then, the four Hurons raced toward them. Uncas and Hawkeye each brought down one Huron. The last two Hurons ran toward the cave.

Hawkeye jumped at one of the Indians with his knife. Duncan went after the other. Hand-to-hand fighting was old work for Hawkeye, but Duncan was new at it. One Huron's hands found Duncan's neck and pressed down hard. But just then a knife flew into the Huron's back, and he released his hold. Uncas had saved Duncan.

"Take cover for your lives!" cried Hawkeye. "The work is but half ended!"

Flashes of rifle fire came across the river.

Chingachgook and Uncas shot back. "Stop firing!" cried Hawkeye. "I've used the last of my gunpowder and bullets. Go to the canoe and get the big powder horn, Uncas. If I know these Hurons, we will need it to the last grain."

The young Mohican did as Hawkeye asked—but it was too late. A Huron had found the canoe. Now he was swimming with it to the other side of the river. When he got to dry land, he let out a shout to signal his success to his friends.

"Well, they do have something to shout about," Hawkeye said. "The best rifle in the world cannot fire without powder."

"What can we do?" asked Duncan.

Hawkeye slowly passed his fingers over his forehead in a way that said everything.

"It cannot be that bad," Duncan said. "We can fight them."

"With what?" Hawkeye asked. "Uncas's arrows? The women's tears?"

"Go to my father," Cora said. "Tell him to come with his men. If he hurries, it may not be too late."

Hawkeye turned to her and smiled. "It is better for a man to die at peace with himself than to live with a bad conscience. How could I leave you behind? What could I say to your father?"

But Hawkeye knew that Cora was right. Without powder, they could not defend themselves *or* the girls. If he and the Mohicans got away, they might find help somehow. Hawkeye took Cora's hand. "I'm afraid you are right, young lady," he said. "It's our only chance. Try to stay hidden. But if the Hurons force you to go into the woods, leave a trail. Break the twigs on the bushes as you pass—so we can follow you later."

Then Hawkeye, Chingachgook, and Uncas jumped into the river. The swift current quickly carried them out of sight.

Cora looked at Duncan. "I know you can swim," she said. "Go with them."

"Cora Munro!" Duncan objected. "No matter what you say, I am staying on this island. I will not leave you here alone!"

Duncan, Cora, Alice, and David were alone. The singing teacher was still sleeping. He didn't know what had happened. And even if he did know, Duncan knew that David would be no help.

Duncan dragged some branches in front of the cave to hide the entrance. "The Hurons won't find us as easily as they think," he said. Just then, a yell

burst into the air. The Hurons were on the island!

"We are lost!" cried Alice.

"Not yet," Duncan said in a quiet voice. "The Hurons may be somewhere on the island, but they have not found us. There is still hope."

More yells soon followed the first. "Hawkeye! Hawkeye!" the Hurons called out as they looked for their hated enemy. Two Indians came close to the hiding place. They even bumped into the branches that hid the mouth of the cave. Duncan could see their feet through the leaves, but the branches did their work. The Indians did not see the entrance. After several minutes, they left.

"They are gone, Cora!" Duncan whispered. "Alice, we are saved!"

Alice smiled, but the hopeful expression on her face disappeared instantly. She cried out in horror, pointing to something behind Duncan.

It was Magua, the bad Indian scout! He had quietly sneaked in through the cave's other opening. Now he stood there glaring at them. His face was twisted with hate.

Duncan fired his pistol at Magua, but he missed. When the rest of the Hurons heard the shot, they rushed into the cave. With a look of triumph on their faces, they dragged Duncan and the others into daylight. And there the frightened captives stood, surrounded by the whole band of triumphant Hurons.

Magua's Plan

Duncan was surprised that the Indians didn't kill them at once. But then he realized the truth. The Hurons were less interested in them than they were in Hawkeye. Magua pointed to the wound he had suffered when Hawkeye shot him. "Where is the one who did this?" he asked.

The Hurons were yelling out Hawkeye's name in a furious chant. "Do you hear?" Magua asked. "The Hurons want Hawkeye's scalp—or they will kill those who hide him!"

"He is gone—escaped," Duncan said.

"Is he a bird that can fly?" Magua roared. "Or did he swim down the river like a fish? You must think the Hurons are fools!"

"Hawkeye is no fish," said Duncan, "but he can swim. He left after he used up all his rifle powder. Why should he stay?"

"Why did *you* stay?" Magua asked him angrily.

"Do you want to lose your scalp?"

"The women cannot swim," Duncan said. "I would not desert them."

For the first time, Magua seemed to believe Duncan. "And the Mohicans?" he asked.

"They are gone, too," Duncan said.

When the Hurons found out that Hawkeye was gone, they raised a frightful yell. One of them grabbed Alice by the hair, as if to scalp her. Duncan jumped at the Indian, but he was quickly knocked down and his hands tied.

The Indians took their captives across the river. There they led the horses from their cover in the woods. Then the band of Hurons divided, taking most of the horses. Magua and five other braves stayed behind with the captives, keeping just two horses for the women.

Duncan helped the two sisters get up on their horses. Following Magua, he walked beside them as they rode west along the trail. The Indians stayed near them at all times, watching them closely. Along the way, Cora tried to leave a trail for Hawkeye. Whenever she could, she bent twigs on the trees she passed. But the Hurons' watchful eyes made this act both difficult and dangerous.

After crossing a low valley, Magua led them up a steep hill. Once at the top, he gave a great sigh and threw himself down under a tree. At last, the group would have a chance to rest.

After a while, one of the Indians went out hunting. He soon came back with a young deer. The five Hurons butchered it and began to eat it right away. They didn't even cook it!

Magua sat apart from them, eating nothing. He seemed to be deep in thought. At last he said to Duncan, "Go get the dark-haired daughter. Say that Magua wants to speak to her!"

Duncan brought Cora to him. Magua rose slowly, standing still and silent for a moment. Then, with a wave of his hand, he signaled Duncan to leave. At first Duncan would not go. But Cora smiled calmly. "Go to Alice and comfort her," she said. "We had better do as the Huron asks."

Then she turned to the Indian. "What would Magua say to the daughter of Munro?" she asked.

Magua laid his hand firmly on her arm. "Magua is a chief of the Hurons," he said. "Before he saw the white man, he lived 20 happy years. Then the French came into our woods. They taught Magua to drink the fire-water, and he became bad—a rascal! The Hurons forced him to leave the land of his fathers. Can Magua help it if his head is not made of rock? Who gave him the fire-water? It was people of your own color."

Cora's pretty face showed some sympathy, but her voice was firm. "Must *I* answer for what some thoughtless white men did to you?" asked Cora.

"Listen!" said Magua. "When the English and the French made war, I went with the English. I began fighting my own people. The old army chief—your father—was the head of the war party. He said he would whip any Indian who drank the fire-water. But the fire-water is the *devil*! Magua could not keep away from it. And what did the Gray-head do to him?"

"He kept his word and did justice by punishing you," Cora said.

"*Justice?*" Magua yelled. "Is it justice to bring evil and then punish others for it? Magua was not himself. It was the fire-water that spoke and acted for him! But Munro would not believe it. He had his soldiers whip Magua like a dog."

He pointed to the scar of an old wound on his chest. "See! When my enemy cut me here, I laughed. I told him that only a woman could give such a little cut. Magua is brave and strong. But

27

the blows of Munro are still hurting me."

"What do you want?" Cora asked.

"Good for good. Bad for bad."

"Would you get even with a man through his helpless daughters?" Cora asked. "Would it not be more manly to meet my father face to face?"

Magua laughed. "And be killed by the rifles of the Gray-head's soldiers? When Magua left his people, his wife was given to another chief. Let the daughter of the English chief stay with Magua now. Let her live in his wigwam forever!"

Cora gasped. These words made her feel sick.

It was all she could do to reply. "What pleasure would Magua find in sharing his cabin with a wife he did not love? It would be better to take money from my father. Then you could buy the heart of some Huron maiden with your gifts."

Magua stared at Cora, his eyes filled with hate. Cora could not bear to look at him.

"No," said Magua stubbornly. "Munro's child will draw Magua's water, hoe his corn, and cook his food. The Gray-head would sleep at home—but his heart would lie within reach of Magua."

"*Monster!*" cried Cora.

Magua waved her away. As Cora ran off, Duncan hurried over to her. He could see that she was angry and afraid. "What happened?" he asked.

But Cora did not want to frighten Alice by telling what had happened. Shaking her head, she decided that it would be best to say nothing.

Magua had now joined the other five Hurons. By this time, they had finished their disgusting meal and lay stretched out on the ground.

Magua spoke to them quietly for a few minutes. Then, at his command, the Hurons jumped up, waving their knives and tomahawks. Yelling fiercely, they ran toward their prisoners.

A Daring Rescue

Duncan jumped between the Hurons and the girls. Magua laughed at this useless show of courage. He invited the Hurons to take their time and make the prisoners suffer. Two strong Indians pulled Duncan away and tied him to one of the trees. Then David, Cora, and Alice were tied to a tree, each in turn.

Alice was so frightened she could hardly stand. If it weren't for the ropes, she would have fallen down. Cora was afraid, too, but she held herself up straight and refused to cry.

"What does the child of Munro say now?" asked Magua. "Is her head still too good for the pillow in the wigwam of Magua? Will she like it better when her head rolls about the hill as a toy for wolves?"

Duncan was frantic. "What does he mean?" he asked Cora, pulling against his ropes.

"*Nothing!* The man is nothing but an ignorant

savage. He doesn't know what he is doing," said Cora.

Magua spoke out in an angry voice. "Shall I send the yellow-haired one to her father? Or will you carry Magua's water and feed him corn?"

Cora felt a surge of disgust that she could not control. "Leave us alone!" she said.

Magua pointed to Alice. "Look!" he said. "She is too young to die. Send her to Munro."

Cora glanced over at her young sister. She saw that the Indian's words had filled Alice with hope. "Is he going to send me home?" Alice asked.

Cora saw that she couldn't hide the truth from her sister any longer. "Alice," she said, "Magua will not kill you if I stay here—as his wife. Speak to me, Alice, my dear sister. Is life to be bought by such a sacrifice? Would you, Alice, be willing to receive it at such a terrible price?"

"No, no, no! Better that we die as we have always lived—together!" Alice cried.

"Then *die!*" shouted Magua. In a fit of rage, he threw his tomahawk at Alice. It landed in the tree next to her head, cutting off some of her hair.

That was too much for Duncan. He pulled against his ropes, snapping the tree to which he was tied. Then he rushed at another Indian who was getting ready to throw a knife at Alice. Both men fell to the ground, the Indian landing on top of Duncan. Duncan could see the sharp blade gleaming in the air. But then he heard the sudden, sharp crack of a rifle. The Indian with the knife fell dead on the faded leaves by his side!

The Hurons stood looking at each other with their mouths hanging open. They knew only one man who could have made such a shot. "*Hawkeye!*" they cried. And sure enough, Hawkeye, Uncas, and Chingachgook came running out of the woods and attacked the Hurons.

Duncan pulled Magua's tomahawk from the tree. He had never used such a weapon before, but his first throw caught a Huron in the face. Now the fight was more even—four against four.

The battle was fast and fierce. Uncas opened up one Huron's head with a strong blow. Knowing that he couldn't hold on for long, Duncan jumped another Indian. But a few seconds later Hawkeye's rifle came swinging down on the Indian's head, killing him instantly.

One of the Hurons threw his tomahawk at Cora. Luckily, it hit the ropes around her and cut through them cleanly. Cora ran to her sister and quickly

began to untie her. But one of the Hurons grabbed her and pushed her to the ground. Then he brandished his scalping knife.

Uncas saw what was happening. He jumped feet first, knocking the Huron down. Then Duncan's tomahawk and Hawkeye's rifle hit the Huron on the skull. Finally, Uncas plunged his knife into the Huron's heart.

Chingachgook and Magua were still fighting. Covered with dust and blood, they rolled over and over on the ground. Then the Mohican had a sudden chance to make a quick, powerful thrust with his knife. Magua fell over and lay still.

Chingachgook got to his feet, a smile on his face. But just then, Magua jumped up and dashed off into the woods.

"He tricked us!" Hawkeye cried. "The coward! Let him go. He is only one man, after all—and he has no rifle or bow."

Uncas ran over to the girls. He took the ropes off Alice and placed her in Cora's arms.

Hawkeye cut the ropes off David. "Now, here's some advice!" he said to the trembling singing teacher. "Forget about the singing for now. Buy a rifle instead—and practice until you can use it well. Then, the next time there is danger, you will be useful."

David held out his thin hand to Hawkeye. "Friend," he said, "thank you for saving me."

Duncan walked up to the two men. "He speaks for me as well," he said to Hawkeye. "But I have been wondering about your return. How is it that we see you back so soon—and without any help from Fort William Henry?"

"It would have taken too long to get there," Hawkeye answered. "You would have been dead long before we could make our way back. So, as soon as we got a good supply of gunpowder, we started to trail you. That way, when you needed us, we would be ready to help."

After resting and eating, they started off for Fort William Henry. By hurrying, the little group of travelers covered a good many miles before the sun set. After another short rest, they set out again and traveled as fast as they could.

They rode many miles without saying a word. Then, without warning, Hawkeye held up his hand as a signal to stop. "Quiet!" he whispered. "I hear someone coming our way."

The men brought up their rifles, ready to fire. But at that moment they heard a man's voice call out to them from the dark. He was speaking in French!

Back at the Fort

Clamping his hand over Hawkeye's mouth, Duncan called out an answer in French. Then he came out of the leafy shadows to within a few yards of the man. They talked for a few minutes. Finally, the man let the group pass, little suspecting that they were the enemy.

"That was a French soldier," Duncan said to Hawkeye. "I wasn't sure I could get away with it. I told him that we were French, too. He had news. General Montcalm and his soldiers are just outside Fort William Henry, ready to attack."

Smiling, Hawkeye said, "I am glad you were here. I don't know a word of French."

"But what will we do?" asked Duncan. "The French are between us and the fort."

Hawkeye thought a moment. "We must go up into the hills for a better view," he said.

Soon they came to the foot of a steep hill. The

climb up was hard work for the horses. But by morning they were so high up they could see for miles around. On each side of them, there were more big hills, one after another. On the other side of the woods, facing Lake Erie, stood Fort William Henry. In the woods near the front of the fort, the white tents of General Montcalm's French soldiers were lined up in rows.

"How many soldiers does Montcalm have?" Duncan cried in amazement. "There are enough tents for 10,000 men."

"Look!" Cora called out, pointing toward the fort. "Riflemen are shooting at the side of my father's house! I cannot bear to be away from him when he is in such danger. Alice and I must get inside the fort to be with Father!"

"There may be a way to get through the enemy lines," said Hawkeye. "I have an idea. This is lake country. The fog will be rolling in soon. Perhaps we can use it as cover."

Duncan helped Cora and Alice on the climb down. By the time they reached the bottom of the hill, a heavy fog had rolled in. They could hardly even see one another! They had to stay close together so no one would get lost.

They silently followed Hawkeye through the thick fog. After some time, they heard some French soldiers talking. Luckily, the fog was so dense that the soldiers did not know they were there.

Hawkeye waited a few minutes before going on. He then led them through the heavy fog for about a mile. Then Alice fell, making a loud noise.

Not far in front of them, a voice called out in English, "Stand ready, men! Wait to see the enemy before you fire!"

The girls knew that voice. "Father! *Father!*" cried Alice. "It's us!"

"Hold your fire!" came the answer. "It is Alice!"

Hawkeye had brought the sisters home. But there was no time to talk. The French were attacking. Colonel Munro sent the girls inside the fort where they would be in less danger. Then he and Duncan hurried back to their men.

The fighting continued for days. The English soldiers fought bravely, but they were greatly outnumbered. Success seemed impossible.

Then a scout told them that another company of English soldiers was nearby. They were under the command of General Webb. Colonel Munro sent Hawkeye to ask General Webb for help.

But Hawkeye was caught trying to get back through the French lines. The French General Montcalm let Hawkeye return to the fort—but he kept the letter from General Webb. After arriving back at the fort, Hawkeye told Colonel Munro that Montcalm wanted to see him.

Munro spoke in a grave voice to Duncan. "General Montcalm is holding a letter that was sent to me from General Webb. I must get that letter. I have to know if General Webb is coming."

"Can I help?" asked Duncan.

"Yes, you can," said Colonel Munro. "Go in my place to meet Montcalm. And get that letter!"

In 10 minutes, Duncan was walking off toward the French camp. To protect himself from enemy attack, he was carrying a white flag. When he got inside the camp, some French soldiers took him to meet with their general.

Duncan was surprised to find Magua in the presence of Montcalm. The Huron glared at Duncan with hate, but General Montcalm was very kind to his visitor. After much talk, however, Montcalm still refused to give General Webb's letter to Duncan. He stubbornly insisted that he would give it only to Colonel Munro.

Later, when Colonel Munro heard about General Montcalm's demand, he was angry. "So he will talk only to me. Well, we *must* have that letter! Send a messenger to tell Montcalm that I am coming. I will go there right away."

It was late afternoon when Colonel Munro came back from the French camp. As he entered the fort, his step was heavy and his face looked sad. He remained silent until he and Duncan were alone. Then he said, "I have read General Webb's letter. He said he could not spare any troops to help us! But the French have more than 10,000 men, Major

Heyward—we cannot win! It is impossible."

Colonel Munro went on to explain that General Montcalm had come up with an offer. The French general had said that he only wanted the fort. He saw no need to kill all the English inside. If the colonel would give up the fort, the English could march away. No one would be hurt.

Colonel Munro did not like it, but he could see no other choice. He knew that dead men were of no use to the king. And he could not bear to put the women and children in any further danger.

The next morning he sadly signed the treaty that turned over the fort to General Montcalm. By the terms of the treaty, the English could keep their arms, their flags, and their baggage. In this way, according to military tradition, they would also be keeping their honor.

7 A Terrible Attack

The next morning, the English were getting ready to leave Fort William Henry. The air was filled with the sound of the French soldiers' drums and horns. Colonel Munro came up to Duncan. His face was weary looking and sad. "Major Heyward," he said, "I must help *all* the women and children get ready to leave the fort. I have no extra time to help my own daughters. Will you help them?"

Duncan was more than willing. He hurried over to Cora and Alice. Although Cora was pale and upset, she was still strong. Alice, on the other hand, was growing weaker. Her puffy red eyes showed how much she had been crying.

"I have come to offer you my help," said Duncan.

"No help is needed," said Cora bravely. "You belong with your men. And listen! Chance has already sent us a friend when he is most needed."

42

Duncan wondered who she was talking about. But he came to understand Cora's meaning when he heard the sound of singing. He followed the sound and found David.

"Hello, David," said Duncan. "I've come to ask you to watch after Cora and Alice on the march. Will you make sure that no harm comes to them? Colonel Munro and I must stay with the men."

David quickly agreed, promising to stay close to the young sisters. "And I'll sing to them along the way," he said with a smile.

Duncan looked on as David helped the two girls. Since there was no special danger in the march itself, he thought they would be fine. Even so, he planned to join them as soon as he had led the men a few miles toward the river.

At last, the English were ready to leave the fort. The soldiers marched out first. Then the sick and the wounded came out riding every available vehicle and horse. The women and children had to travel on foot, following the others. Finally, all had left and the French entered Fort William Henry.

The march was slow and difficult for the English. The little children could not walk fast. Their mothers had to carry them or pull them along. After

a while, even the soldiers had a hard time of it. Many of them were wounded, and all of them were very discouraged and tired.

The troop of English refugees had not gone far when Magua and his Hurons appeared. The Indians watched silently as the soldiers marched by and went deeper into the woods.

Then, as the women and children were passing by, something happened. One of the Hurons noticed a bright shawl worn by one of the women. He tried to grab it from her. In unthinking terror, the woman wrapped her small baby in the shawl, pulling her closer. Then, with an angry yell, the Indian let go of the shawl and tore the screaming baby from her mother's arms.

The little girl's mother cried out, "No! Take the shawl. Give me back my child!"

The Indian looked at the woman and laughed. Swinging the baby by her legs, he dashed her little head against a rock! Then he threw the dead child on the ground and drove his tomahawk into the mother's head! The young woman fell to the ground on top of her child.

At this moment, Magua gave out a wild war cry. More than 2,000 Hurons came from the forest. They began to attack the women and children.

Shocked and terrified, the women scrambled to escape with their children. But the women were knifed, tomahawked, and shot as they tried to run away. Death was everywhere. In minutes, pools of English blood covered the ground.

Hearing the screams, the English soldiers turned back. But the French had not let them take powder for their rifles. So the English soldiers had to fight the Indians with their hands. On all sides there were terrifying shrieks and groans.

David tried to drag Alice and Cora away from

the slaughter. But Alice had fainted.

"Go, David!" cried Cora. "Save yourself." She looked down at her sister. "I must stay with Alice."

In his own way—whether or not he knew how to shoot a gun—David was a brave man. "I am staying, too," he said. "I will try to quiet the Indians with my music."

While the Hurons were yelling, killing, and scalping, David began to sing. His song did not stop the Hurons' wild attack. But the sounds *did* catch the ear of one savage—Magua. When Magua looked around and spotted David, he also saw Cora standing beside him.

Magua pushed his way through the fighting to Cora. "Come," he said. "The wigwam of the Huron is still open. Is it not better than this place?"

"Get away from me!" cried Cora.

Then Magua saw Alice lying on the ground. He picked her up in his arms and ran across the clearing toward the woods.

Without thinking, Cora ran after him. "Put my sister down!" she cried.

David tried to stop Cora. But she pushed him away and ran on. Still singing, David followed her. In a strange way, his singing seemed to protect

Cora. The Indians thought David was insane—and therefore surrounded by the protecting spirit of madness. For that reason, they left Cora alone.

Magua carried Alice to a place where he had hidden two horses. Laying Alice on the back of one of the horses, he made a signal to Cora to climb up on the other.

She obeyed and then held out her arms for her sister. On her face was a look of love that not even the Huron could deny. He placed Alice in her sister's arms and began to lead them away.

David saw that he had been left alone. He didn't understand. It was as if Magua saw him as too worthless even to destroy! He got on the horse Magua had left behind. Then he followed Cora, Alice, and Magua into the dark forest.

Duncan's Plan

Three days had passed since the capture of Fort William Henry. Now a small group of men stood on the battlefield: the two Mohicans, Uncas and Chingachgook; Hawkeye, Colonel Munro, and Duncan Heyward. Death was all around them. The bloody bodies of the dead English soldiers, women, and children lay everywhere. The five men were walking around among the dead, looking for some sign of Cora and Alice.

Just then, Uncas saw something. He raced over to a bush. He tore a tiny piece of Cora's green coat from the branches and waved it in the air. His yells brought the others over to him.

"My children!" cried Colonel Munro. "Where are my dear children?"

Hawkeye was saddened by the father's worry. "Uncas will try to find them," was his short and touching answer.

The men went on hunting for more signs of Cora and Alice. Soon they found another piece of Cora's coat on the branch of a beech tree. And a few minutes later Uncas found some footprints that he could tell belonged to Magua.

Hawkeye led them down the trail into the forest. At first, they found no signs of Alice, but they knew they were following Cora and Magua. Then, after many hours, Uncas found a shining trinket on the ground. Heyward recognized it as a bauble that Alice liked to wear around her neck.

Later, they saw footprints that could belong only to David Gamut. "Good man—he has been faithful to his trust!" Duncan cried. "At least Cora and Alice are not without a friend."

"Yes," said Hawkeye doubtfully. "He will sing for them, all right. But will he be able to defend them? I don't think so."

By now the sky was getting dark. The men spent the night in the woods. The next morning, Hawkeye called the others around him. "Their trail is going north. Magua will stay near the river. If I am right, we will cross their path soon. Follow me, men. We must get going!"

They made good time traveling up the river by

canoe. Soon they made up for Magua's headstart. When they reached Lake George, they took the canoe out of the water. They carefully hid it under a pile of brush in the nearby woods. Then they began trailing Magua over land.

Uncas and Chingachgook were experts at reading the signs of nature. They could always tell if someone had been on the trail recently. Magua, of course, had tried to hide any signs of his trail. But the Mohicans were not fooled. The men followed the trail for many hours.

"I smell Hurons," Hawkeye said at last. "Let's do a little scouting. Uncas, you go to the left. Chingachgook, try that hill on the right. I'll go on following the trail. If anything happens, give the birdcall—three times."

The Mohicans left without saying a word. Colonel Munro sat under a tree to rest, but Duncan was too nervous. He could not sit still, so he went with Hawkeye. They had not gone far when Duncan saw a man off to his left. Duncan could see only the man's back. Like the Mohicans, the man had almost no hair on his head. But attached to that small bit of hair were some bright feathers.

"Hawkeye!" hissed Duncan. "Look on my left!

There's an Indian over there."

Hawkeye looked where Duncan was pointing. "He is no Huron," Hawkeye said. "I don't know what he is. I thought I knew every tribe in this part of the world." Then suddenly, Hawkeye started to laugh. "Ha! I think I know after all! Stay here. I'll go get him."

Hawkeye was not gone long. He soon came back with the man Duncan had thought was an Indian. It was David Gamut!

Hawkeye was still laughing. "Well, Mr. Gamut," he said. "What are you doing here? Are you busy teaching the beavers to sing?"

Before David could answer, Hawkeye put his hand to his mouth and gave three birdcalls. In a few moments the Mohicans and Colonel Munro came running up the trail.

Colonel Munro's eyes grew bright when he saw David. "Thank God!" he cried. "Where are Cora and Alice? Where are my children?"

"I am sorry to say that they are captives of the Indians," David answered. "They are frightened, but they have not been hurt."

"My children are *alive!*" exclaimed Munro. "I shall soon see them!"

"I don't know about that," said David. "Cora has been sent to another tribe. Alice is here among the Huron women—about two miles away."

"Why do the Hurons let you come and go as you please?" Duncan asked. "Why haven't they kept you tied up?"

"Because I sing to them," said David, smiling. "For some reason, my singing makes these wild men behave kindly to me."

Hawkeye laughed. "Do you know why?" he asked. "Your singing makes the Hurons think you are crazy. Indians never hurt a crazy man. They think he has been visited by the Great Spirit."

Then Hawkeye stopped laughing. In a serious voice he asked David, "What about Magua? Where is he?"

"He went hunting for moose today," said David. "I don't know when he will be back."

"Tell us more about the tribe that has Cora," said Hawkeye. "Did you see any pictures of the tortoise in their village? A picture that looked like this?" He pulled aside the folds of Uncas's clothing. There on Uncas's chest was the faint figure of a tortoise, worked in a clear blue tint.

"Yes! *Yes!*" cried David in surprise. "I saw many

pictures of tortoises just like that one."

"They are Delaware," Hawkeye told him. "That may be a help. At one time Chingachgook and the chief of the Delaware were like brothers. They both honor the sign of the tortoise. Cora is better off with them than with the Hurons."

"What can I do to help you get Cora and Alice back?" asked David.

"Go back to the Huron camp. Find out what they are planning to do with the girls. And try to let Alice know that we are here. When you hear my birdcall, come back here."

"I will go with him," said Duncan.

"Are you tired of seeing the sun rise and set?" asked Hawkeye.

"The Hurons did not kill David," Duncan pointed out.

"That is because they think he is a madman and a fool," Hawkeye explained. "With you, it will be quite another story."

"But I too can play the madman, the fool, the hero. I can do anything necessary to save the one I love. I am going, Hawkeye," Duncan said firmly.

Hawkeye looked squarely at Duncan for a long moment. "All right! All right! We will paint you up

like a magician. Perhaps they won't kill you. But I don't like your chances."

Chingachgook brought out the little bag of paints he always carried. He painted Duncan's face, being careful not to paint any signs of war. He made Duncan look like an Indian magician who might be traveling among the tribes.

When Chingachgook had finished, Hawkeye put his hand on Duncan's arm. "You have shown a spirit that I like. You have a warm and brave heart. But believe the warning of a man who tells the truth: *You must use your head.* Every minute that you are in the Huron camp you will be in great danger. If they find out who you are and why you are there, they will take your scalp."

§9 The Race of the Captives

The Huron camp was not far away. Within half an hour, Hawkeye and his party could see some 50 or 60 lodges in the distance. These Indian homes were made of logs, brush, and earth.

As Duncan and David got close to the village, some children saw them and called out. Their cries brought a dozen braves to the door of the nearest lodge. They watched suspiciously as David led Duncan to the biggest lodge. Then they followed the two men inside.

The Huron chief was sitting on the ground inside. He was smoking and talking to some other Indians. After looking Duncan over, he spoke—but in a language Duncan did not understand. Duncan answered him in French. He wanted to fool the Huron chief into thinking he was a friend. Then the chief asked him, "Why have you come here?"

"The great French white father sent me to you,"

Duncan answered. "I am to help those who are sick. I am a great magician."

The chief frowned. He looked as if he did not believe Duncan. "We scalped those English women and children," he finally said. "Is not the French white father angry?"

Duncan forced himself to smile at the chief's terrible confession. "The English are the enemies of the French," he said. "The French white father is happy to see them gone."

"Why does the white magician paint his face?" the chief asked coldly.

"When an Indian chief visits his white brothers, he wears white man's clothes," said Duncan. Then, trying to seem sincere, he made a point of looking straight into the chief's eyes. "So, when I visit you, I paint my face."

Smiles from the Hurons showed that Duncan's answer pleased them. Even the chief seemed pleased. Duncan began to breathe more freely. His hopes of success grew brighter.

Suddenly, a high, shrill yell was heard. The Hurons ran out of the lodge to see what was happening. The air was filled with loud shouts. Duncan left the lodge, too, and stood outside with

the crowd. All the men, women, and children were clapping their hands with great joy.

A Huron war party was coming into the camp. They were bringing with them an Indian captive, his hands tied behind his back.

The sounds that Duncan had heard were called the "death-hello." As the captives came into the camp, the Hurons formed two lines. The men drew their knives. The women picked up clubs and axes. The children lifted tomahawks and rocks.

They were getting ready for the "Race of the Captives." As a terrified captive would try to run between the lines, the Hurons would try to kill him. If he made it to the end alive, they would stop hitting him. Very few men had ever survived. Now the chief signaled for the "death-hello" to begin.

Duncan did not think the Indian could make it. Before he had run five steps, he was covered with blood. Then he was knifed by a Huron and fell to the ground. Duncan thought he had been killed. But the man jumped to his feet. Blood was oozing out of a leg wound, but he kept running.

The Huron standing next to Duncan began swinging his tomahawk as the captive neared them. But just as he threw it, Duncan bumped into him. The tomahawk missed. The captive ran by and made it to the end of the lines.

The blows and yelling stopped. But the quiet was heavy and angry. The captive stood apart, leaning against a lodge pole. He was close enough now for Duncan to see his face. It was Uncas! Just then, a warrior took Uncas by the arm and led him into the main lodge.

As Duncan was trying to think of what to do, the chief saw him. "Come," he said, taking Duncan into the lodge with him. Duncan saw Uncas standing in the center of the lodge, proud and calm.

He gave no sign that they knew each other. That would be too dangerous for both of them.

"The wife of one of my sons is sick," the chief said to Duncan. "Our magician is not making her well. Can you try to make her well?"

"Yes," said Duncan. "I'll do what I can."

Then, as the chief was about to take Duncan to the sick woman, someone else came into the lodge. Looking up, the chief smiled and asked, "Did Magua have good hunting?"

Magua was just returning from his moose hunt. He was about to answer the chief when he looked over and saw Uncas in the lodge.

"Mohican!" Magua cried in surprise. He angrily turned to the chief. "This is my great enemy. Let Magua kill him now."

Magua began to swing his tomahawk over his head. Then he suddenly stopped as if he had just had another idea. "No," he said. "The sun must shine on my enemy's shame. The women must see his fear. Magua will kill his enemy in the morning. Sleep well, Mohican!"

Two Hurons grabbed Uncas and led him from the lodge. Magua left right after that. Duncan felt weak with relief—Magua had not recognized him in his disguise!

Then the chief led Duncan to the sick woman. She was being kept in a cave some distance from the village. Along the way, they met a large black bear. Duncan was uneasy, but the chief explained that the bear was the tribe's magician. He said that the bear would help Duncan heal the woman. So the bear lumbered after them to the cave.

Duncan could see that the woman was close to death. He knew he could not help her. But he put on a show for the chief anyway. He pretended as best he could that he could heal the woman.

After a moment, the chief left Duncan alone with the woman and the bear. Duncan was not afraid, for the bear seemed tame. He knew that Indians often kept bears for pets—but he couldn't help wondering why the chief had said the animal was a *magician*.

10 The Bear Magician

As the bear came closer and closer, Duncan became afraid. He looked around for a weapon but could find none. Then the bear's big paws started to pull at its own head! Suddenly the huge furry head fell to one side. In its place was the face of Hawkeye! He smiled at Duncan.

"Thank heaven, it's Hawkeye! I thought you were a *real* bear," Duncan cried out in relief. "What are you doing here?"

"I've come to get you and Uncas," said Hawkeye. "This bearskin belongs to the tribe's magician. I hit him over the head so I could borrow it for a while. Then I tied him to a tree—so he won't be coming after me very soon. I can go wherever I want in this disguise. Even the chief fears the magician."

"We must act fast," Duncan said. "Uncas will be killed in the morning."

"Not if we can help it," Hawkeye said. "But first,

we need to save Alice. I found out that she's being kept in these caves. In fact, she's in the very next room! I don't want her to see me in this skin. The girl would probably faint from fear. So you must go to her. Tell her that we will get her out of here soon. But take some water from this little stream and wash your face first. All that paint would frighten Alice. She wouldn't know who you are."

Duncan washed his face and crept down the dark passage to the next room in the large cave. Alice was surprised and happy to see him.

Duncan gently took her hands in both of his. But then he felt a light tap on his shoulder and jumped in alarm. Turning around, he saw the dark form and evil face of Magua!

"Huron, do your worst!" cried Duncan, ready to defend himself and the girl he loved.

"Will you speak those brave words at the stake?" asked Magua. "Let Magua see how the white man likes being whipped."

Just then, Hawkeye came into the room. Still wrapped in the bear hide, Hawkeye grabbed Magua in a crushing bear hug. Then he and Duncan tied him up and gagged him.

"Follow me! We must make a push for the

woods right away," Hawkeye said.

"No, we *can't*!" Duncan cried. "Look! Alice has fainted from pure terror. She is helpless."

"Then you must carry her!" said Hawkeye. "Wrap her in those Indian blankets. We'll pretend she is the sick woman. Tell the Indians outside that you must take her into the woods. Say you need to go there to find special medicines."

The plan worked. Soon Hawkeye, Duncan, and Alice were far away from the Huron camp.

Alice soon felt better. "I can walk now," she said.

"Good," said Hawkeye. "Now you two go to the Delaware camp. Colonel Munro and Chingachgook are hiding near there. I must return to help Uncas escape. They'll kill him if I don't. If Uncas and I manage to escape, we'll meet you later."

Duncan and Alice watched as Hawkeye went back toward the Huron lodges. Then they started toward the village of the Delawares.

Hawkeye, still wearing the bearskin of the tribe's magician, got to the camp with no trouble. No one tried to stop him.

But just as he was passing one of the small lodges on the outskirts of the camp, he heard singing. He couldn't believe it. It could only be

David Gamut. Hawkeye hurried into the lodge.

David was shocked when he saw the bear. He jumped up, trembling with fear.

"Don't be frightened, David," laughed Hawkeye as he pulled off the bear's head. "It is only me—pretending to be the magician's bear. Don't worry. Duncan and Alice have escaped. I am here to help Uncas. Will you help me?"

"Yes," said David, still shaking from head to foot. "I'll show you where he is. But how can we possibly save him? Uncas is being watched by five Huron braves. And they are holding him in the big lodge in the very center of the village."

"We must trick them," Hawkeye said, putting on the bear's head again. "Tell the braves that the magician wants to see the Mohican. Trust me, David—I'll do the rest."

At the sight of David and the bear, the five braves stood up. "The magician is here to see the captive," David said. "Let him go in!"

The braves stepped away from the door. One of them made a signal for the bear to go in. But the bear sat down near the door and moved no farther. Then he gave a loud roar.

"He will not go in while you are standing there," said David. "Go away!"

The Hurons were afraid of the magician, so they did what he wanted. They moved aside. But they were still close enough to watch the door to the lodge. Satisfied, the bear got up and slowly entered the lodge. David stood just outside the door.

11 Another Daring Rescue

Uncas was lying in a corner of the lodge, tied up hand and foot. Hawkeye roared fiercely as he walked toward him. He wanted the braves outside to hear it. Uncas was not afraid of the bear. He simply closed his eyes, much as if he were bored. Then Hawkeye made another loud noise. It sounded like the hissing of a snake.

Uncas opened his eyes and looked at the bear. "*Hawkeye!*" he cried in a hoarse whisper.

"Cut his ropes," Hawkeye said to David, who had just then come in.

Hawkeye took off the bearskin and drew a long knife from a pouch hanging at his side. He gave the knife to Uncas. "Five Huron braves are outside. Let us be ready," he said. "Now, Uncas, you must get inside the bear hide. David and I will trade clothes. In the dark I will look enough like him that no one will stop us."

"But what about *me?*" David asked nervously.

"Lie down," said Hawkeye. "It is very dark in here. When they check on you, they will think you are Uncas. It could be a long while before they discover the truth. By that time, we can be at the Delaware camp. When the Hurons do find you, break out into one of your songs. They already think you are a madman, so they will not hurt you. Then, as soon as you can, come to meet us."

Hawkeye and Uncas stepped out of the lodge. Hawkeye was wearing David's clothes. Uncas was wearing the bearskin. The Hurons came toward them. But before they got close enough to see Hawkeye's face, Uncas let out a fierce growl. Surprised and afraid, the Hurons backed away. Uncas and Hawkeye walked right by them and headed toward the woods. Hawkeye even started singing, trying to sound like David.

The five braves watched them leave. Then they sat down in front of the lodge again. A few minutes later, one brave went in to check on Uncas. For some reason he looked closely at the prisoner's face. Seeing David, he let out an angry yell. "The Mohican has escaped!" he cried.

The five braves ran through the village, waking the tribe. Soon the air was filled with noise. Hearing it, Hawkeye and Uncas dashed ahead even faster. They were soon deep in the forest.

By this time Magua had worked free of his bonds. Leaving the cave, he was among the Hurons who went after Hawkeye and Uncas. Knowing that Uncas would be looking for Cora, Magua headed straight toward the Delaware camp.

It was early morning when Magua and his men reached the camp of the Delaware. Magua was surprised to see that Duncan and Alice were there. But he was not at all surprised to find Uncas and

Hawkeye. In fact, he was glad that they were all there together. He hoped that he would be able to convince the Delawares to hand over his enemies to him.

But old Chief Tamenund of the Delawares was a very wise leader. When he looked at somebody, he knew what that person was thinking. Chief Tamenund had never liked or trusted Magua. He knew that the Huron was a coward at heart. But the Hurons were friends of the Delawares. So he had to be respectful and listen to Magua politely.

Magua lied to Chief Tamenund about Hawkeye. "I have come for the dark-haired woman," he said. "But I find my enemies in your camp." Then, pointing to Hawkeye, he continued, "That one is an English scout. He has killed Delaware braves as well as Hurons." Finally, pointing to Uncas, Magua said, "This one is the scout's friend. They are both your enemies. You should kill them."

Three Delaware braves did not wait to hear more. Before Chief Tamenund said a word, they grabbed Uncas. But as they did so, they accidentally pulled his clothing aside. Then, with a sudden cry of surprise, the braves released him! They had seen the blue tortoise on his chest!

Chief Tamenund stood up. "I know that sign! Who are you to wear it?"

"Uncas, the son of Chingachgook," the young Mohican answered.

Chief Tamenund walked over and gently put his hand on Uncas's arm. For a long while he looked into the young Mohican's eyes. "Is it really so?" he asked. "Yes! You look just like your father! Your father and I were as brothers when we were boys. You and your father are the last of the Mohicans. Until now, I thought you were dead. It is a good day that brought you here."

Uncas looked at the chief. "Chief Tamenund," he said, "do not kill Hawkeye. He is my friend."

"What? You should not call such a man a friend," Chief Tamenund said in a scolding voice. "Magua says that he has killed many of my braves."

Hawkeye stepped up to the old chief and looked him in the eye. "It is true that I have killed many Hurons—but never have I killed a Delaware brave," he said. "He that says different is lying."

Chief Tamenund studied Magua's face. "Then has the Huron been lying to me?" he asked.

Magua looked frightened but he pretended to be angry. "The just Tamenund will not keep what belongs to me," said Magua. "These white people and the Mohican belong to *me*!"

The old chief looked back at Uncas. "Tell me, son of my brother, are you Magua's captive?"

"Of course not," said Uncas.

"What about Hawkeye?"

Uncas laughed. "No. Just ask the Hurons who has their magician's bear."

"And the soldier and the woman who came into my camp together?" asked Tamenund.

"They escaped from the Huron camp," Uncas assured him.

"And the dark-haired woman?"

Uncas did not answer.

"She is *mine*!" Magua cried. "Tell him, Mohican. You *know* that she is mine."

"My son is silent," said Tamenund.

"It is so," Uncas said in a quiet voice.

 # A Day
# of Sorrow

Chief Tamenund wanted to help the son of his old friend. But he was a chief and therefore bound by honor to follow the ways of his people. Cora would have to be returned to Magua.

Then Duncan had an idea. "Gold, silver, gunpowder—all that a warrior needs shall be yours. Just return the girl to us."

"No!" Magua snarled, pulling Cora away.

"Wait!" Hawkeye cried. "Take *me* in place of the woman. Just let her go."

Magua stopped and thought about this for a moment. How happy he would be to kill his long-time enemy! But his hatred for Colonel Munro was even stronger than his hatred for Hawkeye. There was no better way of getting even with the colonel than by taking Cora. "No," he said. "Magua will keep the woman."

"Huron!" cried Uncas. "Look at the sun. When

it can be seen over the trees, I will be on your trail."

"I am not afraid," said Magua. He turned his back on the chief and dragged Cora away.

By custom, as long as the Delawares could see Magua, they could not stop him. But once Magua was out of their sight, they could get ready for war. So it wasn't long before a band of Delawares started out for the Huron camp, with Hawkeye and Uncas in command.

On the way they met David Gamut, who had simply walked away from the Huron camp. David quickly warned them that the forests were full of Hurons, led by Magua.

"I'll go to the right with Duncan and my men," said Hawkeye. "Along the way, we'll pick up Colonel Munro and Chingachgook. You take your men toward the left, Uncas. That way, we will trap the Hurons between us."

Both groups moved through the woods. They were as quiet as deer. Hawkeye and his Delawares did not go far, however, before some of the Hurons saw them. Then rifle shots rang out, and one of the Delaware braves fell dead.

"To cover, men!" cried Hawkeye.

The Delawares ran behind trees. Using the trees

as camouflage, they returned the Hurons' fire.

The Delawares were skillful fighters. But they were fighting on the Hurons' homeground—and they were outnumbered two to one! It soon became clear that they were losing the battle.

But just then, the Hurons were attacked from the other side. Colonel Munro, Uncas, and Chingachgook had heard the sound of rifles. They had run to help Hawkeye and his men. The Hurons were surprised when they started losing. Some of them ran away from the battle. The rest fell back to their camp.

Uncas and Hawkeye led their men to the Huron camp. The floor of the forest was covered with dead and wounded men. War cries filled the air.

Magua could see that the fight was lost. Taking one Huron brave with him, he ran to the cave where Cora was being kept. He dragged her outside and started up a steep hill nearby. If he could get over the top, thought Magua, he could get away.

But Uncas and Duncan saw them as they moved up the steep slope. "Cora! Cora!" they cried as they ran after them. Hawkeye followed behind, but no one dared to shoot. Magua and the other Huron knew that Hawkeye would not shoot as long as there was any chance that Cora might be hit.

Cora heard Uncas's voice. "I will go no farther," she said to Magua.

Magua drew his long knife. "Woman," he said, "choose now. The wigwam or the knife of Magua?"

Before Cora could answer, Uncas came leaping from a ledge, as if out of nowhere. He was flying head-first at Magua!

Magua jumped out of the way. But just as Magua jumped, the other Huron grabbed Cora and drove his knife into her heart!

Uncas had missed Magua. Before the brave Mohican could get to his feet, Magua buried his knife in his back. Yet, with his last bit of strength, Uncas again staggered to his feet and killed the brave who had murdered Cora. Seeing this, Magua pressed his knife into Uncas's chest three times. Only then, gazing on his enemy with a look of scorn, did Uncas fall dead at Magua's feet.

As Hawkeye came nearer to him, Magua turned and again started to run up the hillside. But just as Magua reached the top, Hawkeye shot him dead. Magua's body fell off the cliff and dropped 1,000 feet into the valley below.

The next day the Delawares were in mourning.

There were no shouts of success, and no songs of victory were heard.

The lodges were empty. All of the Delawares were gathered around a single spot. All were feeling the same emotion. Each eye looked on the center of the ring. There lay the bodies of Cora and Uncas—ready to be buried.

The Delawares mourned first for one, and then for the other.

Cora was buried on a little hill near a group of young pine trees. In years to come, the pines would shade the spot. Six Delaware girls heaped flowers on Cora's body. Then they covered the marks of the freshly turned earth with leaves. The Delawares sang their song of the dead over Cora's body, and David Gamut sang his own song of goodbye.

Colonel Munro spoke to Chief Tamenund. "I thank you, sir. A sad old man is grateful to you for being kind to my daughter. May the Being we all worship under different names bless you." Then he turned to Duncan. "Our duty here is ended," he said. "Let us leave now."

Colonel Munro headed the party. Alice was carried on a closed litter made for her by the Indians. The sound of her low sobs was the only clue that she was lying inside. Duncan and David rode behind Alice. Soon all the white people but Hawkeye had left the Delaware camp.

Now, sadly, the time had come to bury Uncas. Chingachgook spoke. "Why do we weep? A young man has gone to the happy hunting grounds. He has filled his time with honor! He was good. He was brave. He was needed in the other world, and he has been called away. As for me, the father of Uncas—my race is gone. I am alone."

"No, no!" cried Hawkeye. "You are not alone. He was your son, but *I* loved him, too. We will walk the same trail, you and I. The boy has left us for a time—but you are not alone, Chingachgook."

Chingachgook grasped the hand that Hawkeye offered him. Then the two men bowed their heads. Hot tears fell to their feet, watering the grave of Uncas like drops of falling rain.

Chief Tamenund lifted his voice in a mournful prayer. "My day has been too long. This morning the son of Chingachgook was happy and strong. Now we must bury him. I have lived to see the last warrior of the wise race of the Mohicans."